A Tale of Christmas Past:

A Time-Travel Romance Novella

By Katelyn A. Brown

Copyright

Table of Contents

Title Page

Copyright

Dedication

Prologue

Chapter 1

Chapter 2

Chapter 3

Chapter 4

Chapter 5

Chapter 6

Chapter 7

Chapter 8

Chapter 9

Chapter 10

Epilogue

A Note From the Author

Dedication

For you, mom. Thank you for always encouraging me in my creative pursuits and showing me what courage looks like in the face of trial. I hope I've written something you would be proud to read. Love you forever.

Chapter 1

Avery Lawson watched the minutes slowly tick by on the clock, eager for her last class of the day to end. Her university classmates shifted in their seats and scrolled aimlessly though their phones, not even bothering to conceal them underneath the desks. Despite the restlessness of the students, Professor Keegan insisted on droning on and on about business ethics, determined to impart some small bit of knowledge before Thanksgiving break. Finally, he relented, seeing it for the lost cause it was, and dismissed the class.

Gratefully, Avery gathered up her laptop and books, shoving them into her bag. Other students began chattering excitedly about going home for the holiday and the break from classes. As she slipped past a blond girl talking animatedly to her friend about taking her boyfriend home to meet her parents, Avery sighed and escaped the crowded room. On her way to the parking lot, she thought about how different she was from the other students at the small Kansas university.

At twenty-three, the college senior certainly wasn't ancient, but at times Avery felt years older than the other students. Life had forced her to be. During her freshman year, at only eighteen years old, she had lost both her parents in a car accident. Sometimes she still couldn't believe it; she had been incredibly close to her mom and dad. As an only child with no other living relatives nearby, she had pretty much been on her own since then.

When she first began college, Avery had embraced her new freedom and social circle, becoming fast friends with the kids in her dorm and classes. The first semester had flown by, and before she knew it, the second semester was half over. But the week after spring break, her world shattered. She remembered getting the phone call and driving, half-blinded by tears, to the hospital. But it was too late. Both of her parents were gone, and she hadn't even gotten to say goodbye.

Family friends had attempted to reach out to her, as did her own school friends, but the remainder of Avery's first year of college passed in somewhat of a numb, detached blur. Hollow platitudes such as "Everything happens for a reason" and "God has a plan" never comforted her, and she hated when people said them to her.

Avery withdrew from others, even while telling herself to snap out of it. The only comfort she found was in her own independence. She secured housing and a job for herself, moving out of the dorms and into an apartment at the end of the spring semester.

lunch. Dressed in old jeans, a hoodie and warm boots, soon she was out the door and driving to the museum.

She couldn't help but smile at the thought of Agnes, the elderly woman who ran the museum. Aggie had taken Avery under her wing from the moment she had walked in the museum to answer the "help wanted" sign in the window, and was the one person Avery let into her solitary world. Aggie was a warm, grandmotherly type of woman, but she was also incredibly blunt and didn't sugar-coat things. She had been after Avery to let go of her bitterness for the past five years and make her peace with the Lord, to no avail.

The way Aggie put it, Avery was only letting it keep her captive and from living the life she was made for. She made it sound so simple. Avery just gritted her teeth and ignored her when their conversations took that turn, and Aggie would drop the subject. *I'm not heartless,* Avery thought. *I'm still a good person...I just don't want to hear about how great God is when my life completely sucks.* For the most part, Agnes and Avery worked companionably. The old woman was really the closest thing Avery had to a friend, and she appreciated Aggie's consistency.

The temperature had dropped even further, and Avery hugged her coat close. Clouds had rolled in and blocked the miniscule heat the sun had offered that morning. She almost wished Aggie would be at the museum today, both for the warmth of conversation and the steaming coffee and Danish she often brought with her. Aggie had generously invited Avery to spend the holiday with her family, but Avery had declined. She was a private person and didn't relish the thought of forcing a smile all weekend around strangers. She preferred to be miserable alone.

It was a lonely day, dry with cold wind whipping her long hair into a tangle and stinging her face as she hurried from her parking space to the row of storefronts that ran along the deserted street. The faded green door with window displays on either side led to the museum. Avery fumbled with her keys and finally found the right one, grateful to get out of the freezing air.

Avery blinked in the sudden darkness of the large room and reached to turn on the overhead lights. She passed the exhibits that showcased different eras of Kansas history, from abolitionist and pro-slavery raids to life as a pioneer. Rounding a corner and a display of veterans' memorabilia, she made her way to the back room where they kept new items that needed to be organized before being put on the main floor. She soon saw the new inventory Aggie had told her about. A large trunk was set in the middle of the room. It looked to be at least a hundred years old, if not more.

Excitement rising in her, Avery gathered her supplies and went to open the chest. There was something about touching these living pieces of history that she always anticipated eagerly. She wondered about the lives of the people who had actually owned the items and what had become of them.

Carefully unlatching the lid, she lifted it to expose the contents of the trunk. Avery gingerly pulled out a faded patchwork quilt. Underneath it was an

Chapter 3

A very gently stroked the leather binding of the journal, worn thin with time and use. She felt a thrill of anticipation. Wanting to read it then and there, she forced herself to wrap the journal in paper and delicately tuck it into her tote bag before she finished closing up the museum for the evening. It was getting dark and the first snow of the year was beginning to fall, so she needed to be on her way home.

She knew Agnes wouldn't mind her taking the artifact with her as long as it was returned in the same condition. Just to make sure, she dialed Aggie's number on her cell phone as she locked the door and hurried out to her car.

No answer. Aggie was no doubt busy with her visiting children and grandchildren. Avery tapped out a quick text message and sent it to Aggie, explaining the secret compartment in the trunk and the journal she had found there while she waited for the car to warm.

When she was finally home in her cozy apartment, Avery settled in for the evening. She turned on the end table lamp and pulled out Kathleen's journal. Even though Kathleen was long gone by now, Avery still felt a little pang of guilt at reading another woman's private thoughts. Still, her curiosity got the better of her as she opened the yellowed pages and began to read.

April 25, 1870

Our journey has finally begun! Jacob and I are on our way to our new home in Kansas—free land and a fresh start at our very own farm. I'm excited and bone weary at the same time. Walking alongside the wagon from dawn to dusk and cooking over a campfire every meal sure does take the starch out of me some days, and we still have so far to go. Still, I'm determined to keep a record of our adventure, as we call it. Mother gave me this journal before we left Ohio, telling me that someday I would want to look back on this time.

The Lord has been good to us on this first week on the trail. Nobody has gotten sick or injured, and the rains have been light enough this spring that we have crossed the rivers without much difficulty. I pray that things go this smoothly the whole trip, although I think Jacob is eager for a bit more excitement. I'm sure it will come soon enough, but for now I'll be thankful for everyone's good health and safety. I'm off to bed now. Morning comes very early these days.

Avery read on, through Kathleen and Jacob's move to Kansas (which did have its share of scares and mishaps, such as finding a snake in the flour sack—Avery shuddered at the thought—and another family's wagon being swept away while crossing a high river) to setting up a homestead once they arrived.

Avery was amazed at the amount of work the

Chapter 4

A very woke to a strange odor. *Why does my apartment smell like the state fair?* The intrusive thought came to her as she squeezed her eyes shut more tightly, hoping to fall back asleep. She rolled over, trying in vain to find a more comfortable position. Her bed felt hard as a rock and something sharp poked irritatingly into her skin. Frustrated, her eyes finally flew open. In wide-eyed shock, she took in her surroundings.

Gone was her room with the cozy full-size bed, white painted dresser and print of Van Gogh's *Starry Night* on the wall. There was no teal curtain-clad window overlooking the street or phone on her bedside table. What Avery *did* see was, in fact, a rugged barn constructed of wood, an enormous cow peering over a stall at her with curious eyes, and looking down, the pile of coarse straw and packed earth in which she was lying.

What in the world? Avery jumped up, alarm radiating through her entire body. She whirled around, bits of straw flying everywhere and sticking to her clothes. Her clothes! When she had gone to bed, she had been wearing her usual t-shirt and pajama shorts. Now, she was attired in a long, old-fashioned emerald green woolen dress with a cream shawl over her shoulders and completed with black boots. *I must be dreaming,* Avery thought to herself. *That's right; all that reading about Kathleen's life has made me dream that I am living in the 1800s. But why does it feel so real?* There was none of that fuzzy, dream-like quality to what she was experiencing. Everything was crystal clear.

Confused, she absentmindedly began brushing the straw from her skirt. As she did, she spotted a large trunk in the corner of the stall in which she was standing. Avery did a double take. Why, if she didn't know better...quickly approaching the chest, she gave it a once-over and felt her stomach lurch. It was the same trunk she had emptied out in the museum, only now it looked about a century and a half newer. And there, lying on top of the open trunk, was Kathleen's journal.

Thinking this couldn't possibly be real, Avery picked up the journal and thumbed through it. The pages were more white than yellow, giving it a much newer appearance. She discovered that all the entries were there, down to the very last one.

She slipped the journal into her pocket and exited the stall, stepping into the main area of the barn. The walls were covered with nails and hooks on which old-fashioned tools were hung, many of the same types that were on display in the museum. The large barn door was open, and as Avery approached it, she could

rule it out entirely—his gaze flicked to the woman's eyes again—but he forced himself to be skeptical. He'd need some answers first. Clearing his throat, Jake extended his hand.

"I'm sorry, my manners...I'm Jacob Cole. Apparently, you've already met Elizabeth and Caroline, and this is my son, Andrew." The little boy smiled shyly. He had his father's dark hair, but the same pale blue eyes as Caroline.

"Avery Lawson," she replied in a soft voice. Jacob raised his eyebrows at the unique name.

"Um, I'll make some coffee...why don't you have a seat?" Jake gestured to the table and busied himself with kitchen preparations. He didn't want to look at the woman who was stirring up things inside him he hadn't felt for a long time. He had barely looked at another woman since Kathleen died, burying himself in running the farm and caring for his children. But the attractive Miss Lawson made his pulse quicken and his stomach turn in knots. He knew he'd never met her before, yet there was something almost familiar about her. Attempting to place the mysterious stranger was something akin to trying to remember a dream after awaking; almost there and then it slipped away.

∞∞∞

Avery couldn't believe this was happening. There, not five feet in front of her, stood Jacob Cole. She felt she would have known him anywhere, with the tall frame and dark hair. He had light, honey-brown eyes, just as Kathleen had described in her journal. She absentmindedly rubbed the hand he had touched when he introduced himself. It had felt like a jolt of electricity shooting up her arm as she shook his rough hand, and her fingers still tingled. This was the most bizarre experience of her life and she was having trouble believing it was reality.

She sat at the table and watched the man boil water and gather mugs, smiling nervously at the three little faces that expectantly eyed the two adults. Kathleen's children were precious, but the rugged, handsome man before her made her just as nervous as she seemed to make him.

What in the world was she doing here? She was stranded in the nineteenth century with no money, belongings, or conceivable way to get home. She hoped he would offer her a job, because Avery had no idea what to do in the peculiar situation in which she found herself.

Steaming mugs in hand, Jake approached the table while telling the children to go play in their bedroom. They began to protest, but he quieted them with a stern look. The three of them marched upstairs, Lizzie dragging Caroline along by the hand.

"So, Miss Lawson, are you sure you're all right? Have you passed out before?" Jacob inquired about her wellbeing before discussing the job possibility.

"Oh, I'm fine...I was just startled, I suppose." Avery glossed over the incident. Taking a sip of coffee, she nearly spat out the bitter, gritty liquid. It was defin-

and dry, but she couldn't imagine living that way.

Avery recalled from Kathleen's journal that they had lived in this house for several years while they established the farm. While it wasn't uncommon for a log cabin such as this to remain the permanent family home, Jake had been determined to build a beautiful house for his wife. She had written of her joy when they moved to the larger house after Andrew was born.

Kathleen had planned to maintain the cabin, perhaps for a farm or ranch hand if they became successful, or a place for someone to board who had nowhere else to go. Avery smiled grimly to herself, thinking how ironic it was that *she* was the boarder who now occupied the cabin.

Shaking off her musings, Avery pushed up her sleeves and began the work of cleaning the cabin. Jacob had given her the day to get settled in, and she would start her new job first thing in the morning. She had no idea what she was getting into, but then again, she really didn't have a choice.

Avery had no idea how, or when, she could get back home. The thought was downright terrifying, but she took a deep breath and tried to concentrate on one task at a time, and right now she needed to get this place cleaned up. There would be no sleep for her tonight if it remained in this state.

Avery decided to clean the windows first. She needed decent natural light to keep her sanity. She found a bucket, a few old cloths and a bar of soap, and set to work. Jake had shown her the hand-dug well on the way to the cabin, so she set off with her bucket and sheer determination. Drawing water from the well was inconvenient, but at least she didn't have to hike to the creek. Kathleen had mentioned in the journal that they had used the nearby water source until the well was complete.

Returning to the cabin, she shaved a few pieces off the bar of soap with a knife and stirred them around the water, soaked a cloth in the solution and attacked the windows. By the time the windows were cleaned, and she had retrieved fresh water, Avery began to feel better. She was in the middle of dusting the table and cupboards when a knock sounded at the door.

"Come in," she called, and Jacob entered, his arms laden with logs. "Thought you could use a fire," he said, smiling warmly. It looked as though he hadn't shaved in weeks, and Avery tried to ignore how his scruffy appearance actually seemed to enhance his good looks.

"Of course, that would be great." Avery mentally kicked herself for being an idiot. With her adrenaline pumping on overtime, she hadn't even realized how chilly the cabin was. Now she shivered and rubbed her hands together, eager for the warmth the fire would provide. Avery carefully watched his process, so she'd know how to light the fire herself next time.

"I was in such a hurry to clean that I completely forgot," she said absently.

Jacob was busily arranging kindling, but then he paused and looked around the room. "Sorry the cabin's in such a state. I haven't been in here since...for a long time, and it's gotten a mite run-down."

Within a few minutes, Jacob had a fire roaring in

I guess. I haven't set foot here in over a year."

To a stranger, he would have appeared cryptic. Unbeknownst to Jacob, though, Avery knew exactly what he was talking about. If her math was right, Kathleen had died in October the previous year. Kathleen had helped him build this cabin and given birth to both Lizzie and Andrew here.

This was the place they retired each evening after long days on the farm, the place they whispered their hopes and dreams to each other late in the night. They cried and laughed and welcomed their first friends and neighbors over for a meal at the rickety table. Avery reminded herself that she shouldn't know all this, and felt guilty for the intrusion of which he was unaware.

Jacob took a deep breath, nodding toward the end of the bed. "Since you don't have any belongings with you, you're welcome to the things in that trunk. It belonged to my wife."

"I'm sorry for your loss," Avery whispered, her bright green eyes brimming with unshed tears. Jacob shook his head and looked away. He finally stepped though the door and set the tub down.

"If you'll hand me those pails, I'll fetch some water for you."

"Thank you," Avery replied. Giving him one of the buckets, she took the other one, saying, "I'll come with you."

He insisted, so she began heating the water in the large pot over the fire as he brought it to her. It took several trips back and forth to the well. Once she had enough, he helped her light a few candles and an old-fashioned oil lamp. He then lifted his warm, light brown eyes to hers.

"Be seein' you in the morning, then."

"Thank you again, Mr. Cole, for everything," Avery tried to remember the correct name to call him according to what was considered proper. It turned out to be unnecessary, though. His face slipped again into the easy smile that was becoming familiar.

"Call me Jake," he said, putting his worn hat back on his head as he slipped out the door. He touched the brim of it, tipping it toward her before turning to leave.

Avery watched his retreating back and felt her heart squeeze. Even though she had only just met him, she guiltily felt as if she knew him too well, thanks to her snooping in Kathleen's journal. Jake was obviously still grieving for his wife, but he appeared to take life's turbulence in stride. He seemed to accept the bad along with the good, with a gritty determination so characteristic of a pioneer.

The Jake Kathleen had written about was funloving and adventurous. Life may have forced him to deal with hardships, but Avery felt as if the essence of his personality and character remained intact. She wondered why, as she watched him enter the white house, she was overcome with an urge to wrap her arms around him and tell him everything would be okay. She wanted to see him smile again.

they walked on it. There were red gingham curtains on the windows and colorful rag rugs on the floor, giving the home a cozy feeling.

The house wasn't pristine, but Avery supposed that was to be expected with Jake being a single parent and having all the responsibilities of the farm. Blankets and clothing were scattered in a few odd places, and the dishes were washed but not put away, cluttering the worktable in the kitchen.

Lizzie informed her that Drew and Caroline were still sleeping and that her father was in the barn doing the morning chores. He would be back soon for breakfast.

"Well, I guess I should get started." Avery squared her shoulders and approached the kitchen. She eyed the old-fashioned stove dubiously. In the twenty-first century, she actually wasn't a bad cook, but she wasn't so sure of her abilities with this wood stove and oven. She had managed to heat water last night without too much trouble, but breakfast would be another matter entirely.

Turning to Lizzie, she asked, "What do you normally like for breakfast?" Lizzie rattled off their usual fare. Avery thought the flapjacks sounded good, but she felt doubtful of her ability to make them. Back home, she was used to making pancakes with the boxed mix that said, "just add water!"

She found a basket of eggs settled into a corner, and Lizzie showed her the crocks containing flour, sugar, oats and butter. "Do you have any cookbooks or recipes?" Avery wondered.

Lizzie furrowed her brow, as if she expected Avery to know something as simple as how to make breakfast. She pointed out a small book. Opening it, Avery saw that the recipes were hand-written, the first few by an unfamiliar hand. *Perhaps Kathleen's mother?* Soon the handwriting changed to Kathleen's familiar script. The recipes were in no particular order, so she skimmed until she found flapjacks. The ingredients were listed but there were no instructions beyond that. *Hmm, maybe tomorrow,* Avery thought, snapping the book shut.

"You want me to help you, or should I get the little'uns ready?" Lizzie stood there, looking worried. Avery straightened up, determined to succeed in making breakfast.

"You go on upstairs, sweetie." She thought she might do better without an audience. Grabbing a cast-iron pot, spoon, and the container of oats, Avery decided to try making oatmeal instead. Could she really mess up something with only two ingredients? She stirred oats and water together and placed the pot on the stove. But how could she control the temperature? The fire didn't seem hot enough, so she added more wood and soon it was blazing. The oatmeal boiled and she began to stir it. She left it to cook and decided to try making eggs along with it.

Jake rested his head against the milk cow's warm

banging a wooden spoon on various pots and pans, it was time to eat again. Jake joined them for lunch but didn't linger, as he had to get to the Johnson farm to borrow a tool he needed.

Avery found out Drew was extremely accident prone as he broke a dish in the morning and nearly set the house on fire in the afternoon. He had taken it upon himself to stir up the coals wildly and several were flung across the room. He was reserved around Avery and looked at her guiltily after each incident, but he was sweet and affectionate, and she couldn't be mad at him.

Caroline was turning out to be a little fireball. The child was never still, and she was nearly always on the run. She was something of an escape artist and kept disappearing, only to be found in random places around the house. She seemed particularly fond of climbing the banister and trying to slide down it.

"Does she ever slow down?" Avery asked the older two.

"Not really. Pa said she never 'started walking.' One day she just up and ran and hasn't stopped since," Lizzie explained. "She usually naps after lunch, though."

Avery breathed a sigh of relief when the little girl finally fell asleep after an hour of putting her back in bed every two minutes. She had been frustrated and nearly at her wit's end when Caroline had finally gone to sleep with Avery stroking her blond curls. She looked so sweet and peaceful that Avery felt her agitation melt away, replaced by the fierce protectiveness she had felt last night.

Lizzie was her chatty little helper. Avery admitted to her, while the younger ones slept, that she could use some help in the kitchen. Luckily, Drew had gone to bed without complaint and crashed quickly.

"He likes to sleep," Lizzie filled in. Lizzie was a good teacher and soon they had a vegetable stew simmering on the stove and were cutting out biscuits on the table. The biscuits weren't very pretty, but the stew smelled nice.

"Just remember to keep this fire low," Lizzie instructed. "And the stew will be good and ready in a few hours." There were no kitchen catastrophes at dinner, other than the biscuits being slightly over-done and the stew under-seasoned. But it was edible at least, and Avery hoped she'd get a little better each time she used the old stove.

After supper, Jake attempted to relax in the rocker by the fire, but the children pestered him with cries of, "Bull ride! Bull ride!" until he relented and sank to all fours on the floor. Avery smiled from the kitchen, where she was finishing up the dishes.

"I fear, Miss Lawson, that I'm about to ruin my dignity here." Laughing, he let Caroline hop on his back, and he pranced and bucked around until she bounced off onto a small pile of cushions. Each one had several turns, until Jake collapsed on the floor in defeat.

"I think it's about bed time!" he declared, gasping for breath. "Your pa's getting too old for this!" The kids groaned, but eventually all trooped upstairs. Avery helped the girls into their nightgowns and made sure

"And what about you, Miss Lawson?" Jake stood next to Henry, twirling the reins. "Are you gonna ride?"

"No, thanks," Avery replied quickly.

"Don't you ride?" he pried.

"I've ridden a horse before, yes," she said, not adding that she had been on a horse exactly once in her life, on the pony rides at the state fair as a child. It wasn't that she was afraid, but she didn't really want an audience when it became obvious just how inexperienced she was.

"Come with me, then. I'll show you around the farm," Jake offered.

"Really, that's all right," she said. She tried to turn him down gracefully. "I should be getting back to the house to start lunch, anyway."

Jake's eyes twinkled and his mouth twitched mischievously. Avery suspected he was about to be ornery, and her stomach churned nervously.

∞∞∞∞

Jake worked the reins over in his hands, thinking. He was proud of his homestead and the surrounding countryside, and he really did want to share it with Avery. And he didn't mind wounding her pride a bit to get his way.

"Chicken," he goaded.

"Excuse me?" Her green eyes sparked, just the reaction he was hoping for.

"You heard me," he said, keeping a straight face.

"Oh, that's really mature, *Mister* Cole. We're resorting to name calling now? That's a fine example for your children." A hint of a smile broke through, a clue that she was onto his game.

Caroline was dragging a stick through the dirt, oblivious to what was going on around her. But the older two watched the exchange with interest. They were used to the teasing nature of their father and waited to see how it played out. Jake shrugged and began to turn away.

"Fine then, I mean if you're too scared..."

"I am *not* scared," Avery replied. Then she lifted her chin and stomped toward Daisy, the mare Caroline had been riding. Jake winked at Lizzie and Drew, who grinned back at him.

"How am I supposed to get on this thing?" Avery asked as she stood next to the horse.

"Exactly how many times have you ridden?" Jake inquired.

"Um, once?" she admitted. Jake was surprised.

"How is that possible?" he asked. She turned and smiled wryly at him.

"I think I've said it before; my home is a lot different than yours."

Must be a city girl, Jake thought. She sure was mysterious sometimes. Just when he thought he had her figured out, she went and surprised him again. He led her over to Henry, instructed her on how to mount the horse, and then swung up behind her.

"What are you doing?" she choked out. Her voice sounded suspiciously high.

∞∞∞

Avery wondered what had gotten into her. She and Jake had only known each other a few days and were already joking like old friends. She felt more light-hearted than she had in years. Jake had to get back to his work after they ate, but Avery watched him out the window, thinking it was one of the best days she'd had in a long time.

∞∞∞

The next morning, Avery hurriedly readied for the day. Jake was already out milking when she reached the house, and together she and Lizzie made a some-what-edible breakfast. She bravely tried flapjacks this time. She was doing quite well until the fire burned low and she added too much wood at once, burning the outsides of the last two batches while the insides were still raw. She tried her hand at frying the last of the eggs in the basket. A few of the yolks ended up broken and most of them were mangled from her poor attempt at flipping them in the pan. There wasn't a decent one in the bunch.

Stick to scrambling, Lawson! Avery mentally scolded herself. Just then, she heard a thump and a tumble, followed by a cry. Avery ran quickly to the bottom of the stairs, where Drew was lying in a heap. She pulled him up into her lap and checked to make sure nothing was broken. Thankfully, the extent of the damage only seemed to be a scrape to the shin and a banged elbow. There was sure to be a few bruises tomorrow, but at least he hadn't hit his head. Avery was holding him and whispering calm words of reassurance when Jake entered the house.

"Whoa!" he called, quickly pulling the cast-iron skillet off the stove to remove the last batch of eggs, which had started to burn and smoke. He lifted an eyebrow to the pair at the bottom of the stairs.

"You all right, son?" he asked Drew.

"Yes, Pa," Drew stood up.

"No worries—just a scrape," Avery said, running her fingers affectionately through the boy's hair as they walked to the kitchen together.

Watching Avery put her arm around Drew, Jake felt his stomach turn in a way that was becoming entirely too familiar where Avery was concerned. Admittedly, she was a pretty bad cook, but he found he didn't mind so much. The way she lovingly cared for his children more than made up for her lack of domestic skill.

"Sorry about the eggs," she said. "But I'm starting to figure this old girl out!" she joked, patting the stove. Drew eyed the pancakes cautiously, and then nodded.

"Might be able to eat your cooking today," he said quietly, and the adults chuckled at his honesty. Lizzie,

"I've, uh, decided that this trial business is over. How'd you like this to be a full-time job?"

"Really?" Avery asked. "Of course—thank you!" Even if she had anywhere to go, which she didn't, she would have chosen to stay. She was becoming very attached to the Cole clan. Until Caroline was safe and she could figure out a way to get home, she was staying with them.

"Yep, I think I'd have a mutiny on my hands if I sent ya packin', and I can't have that," Jake quipped, jerking his head toward the back of the wagon where the children were snuggled together, sound asleep despite the jostling of the wagon.

"I see, so it's all about self-preservation," Avery lifted an eyebrow at him sardonically, while inwardly feeling a pang of guilt that she *would* have to leave them, if and when she ever found a way back to the twenty-first century.

"Exactly, Miss Lawson, exactly." Jake grinned.

"You know, you can just call me Avery," she replied, suddenly wanting very much to hear him say her real name. No more of the stuffy-sounding 'Miss Lawson.' Jake studied her a moment, his expression unreadable in the darkness.

"All right, then. Avery it is," he said. As she'd suspected, it did funny things to her insides to hear it.

Jake meant it when he said he'd have mutiny on

his hands if Avery left. His children were the happiest he'd seen them in a very long time, and it surprised him how quickly she'd carved out her own place in their world.

The past year had been the hardest of his life. He could handle the busy days, which were so full of chores and children he scarcely had time to think. But the evenings were much too quiet after the kids were in bed, and at those times he couldn't hide from his loneliness.

Jake could admit to himself that he was glad the lady had agreed to stay. It had been too long since his home possessed the warmth a woman brought to it, and Avery had become more of a friend in the last week than an employee.

Not to mention, she's nice to look at, he thought to himself, glancing at her sideways. The moonlight glinted off her dark waves and her emerald eyes sparkled when she smiled at him. His pulse quickened and he found himself wishing she'd snuggle closer to him for warmth, instead of shivering under the coarse, heavy blanket. He shook himself mentally, dragging his eyes back to the trail and the team of horses.

The woman at his side was still downright perplexing at times. She hadn't opened up about the peculiar circumstances that had brought her to his farm. Jake was relying purely on his judgment of character with this one. She seemed to be a friendly, honest and hard-working woman, but at times she said or did things that he found odd. Sometimes she got very quiet, with a faraway look in her eyes, mingled with sadness. He wondered if she'd ever trust him enough to reveal her past to him, and open possibilities to a future as more than just his housekeeper.

He couldn't believe he was entertaining such thoughts, even in the safe recesses of his mind. There was a time, not so long ago, when Jake was certain he would never again look at a woman with romantic notions. However, that was becoming more difficult for him to believe what with the lovely, mysterious distraction sitting next to him.

∞∞∞

The next day was Saturday. While the children played, Avery rushed about the kitchen, doubling recipes so they would have leftovers the next day. Once she finally had her lumpy bread dough in the oven and meat and vegetables simmering on the stove, Avery poured herself some coffee and collapsed into a kitchen chair.

She winced as she took a bitter drink and thought, not for the first time, that she needed to come up with a better idea for her caffeine fix. She looked up as Jake entered the house, bringing a blast of cold air in with him. He poured himself a cup and joined her at the table.

"Tomorrow's Sunday," he began. "Will you be joinin' us for church services? We'll leave right after breakfast," Jake said.

Avery thought for a moment. *Could I really bring*

myself to visit the church here? she wondered. Part of her was very curious about the pioneer church, while the other part of her was filled with anxiety. She balked at the idea of being the subject of town gossip. *I don't think I'm quite ready for that.*

Pretending that the pots on the stove suddenly needed her attention, Avery stood and turned away as she answered him.

"No, thanks. I think I'll stay here while you all go."

"Suit yourself," he replied. "You're always welcome if you change your mind."

Jake stood and moved next to her, stirring the other pot. Avery forced herself to meet his eyes. The same caring warmth was there, along with what looked like concern. She had a feeling he really wanted her to go, but she appreciated that he didn't push the issue.

"Thank you. I'll keep that in mind," she said. He smiled, patting her shoulder in a friendly gesture, before downing his coffee and heading back outside.

∞∞∞

"I think it's 'bout time we found ourselves a Christmas tree," Jake said over breakfast a few days later.

The children cheered with excitement, but Avery stiffened a bit as she turned to clear away the dishes.

Even as the warmth of the Cole homestead slowly thawed her heart, Avery couldn't muster much excitement at the prospect of Christmas decorating. Once it had been her favorite holiday, but in recent years, it only represented loneliness and a reminder of what she'd lost. She missed her mom and dad the most at Christmas.

Christmas had been her mother's favorite holiday. The leftover Thanksgiving turkey had scarcely began cooling in the refrigerator when her mom began filling their home with music and decorations of the season. The Lawson family had certainly not been rich, and Avery's parents were very giving people at any time of the year, but never more so than in December. It had been a special time of good cheer and generosity for her family.

Strange as her situation was, Avery realized the Coles were the closest thing to family she'd had in a long time. Not wanting to disappoint the children, she pasted a smile on her face and turned back to them, hoping to make theirs a happy day.

An hour later, the five of them trooped out the front door and across the field to a place where the trees grew more thickly. Caroline's hand was firmly tucked in Avery's as Jake carried the axe and Lizzie and Drew raced ahead of them. They began to rush from tree to tree, looking for the perfect one. Drew was most concerned about size and shape, while the adults laughed out loud at Lizzie. She had taken to sniffing each tree to find the "perfectest-smelling one," she'd declared.

They finally all agreed on a plump, filled-out cedar tree that was just a bit shorter than Jake. Avery made sure all of the children stayed clear, especially

Drew, who couldn't be trusted around sharp objects, as Jake wielded the axe and chopped the tree down in a few smooth motions.

Avery wondered at the primitive part of herself that marveled at the man's strength. She liked watching him cut down the tree, and she stared as he slung the axe back over his shoulder and dragged it back to the house with the other hand. *Come on, Lawson, you're an enlightened, twenty-first century female, not a cave woman!* she scolded herself, hurrying to catch up with Drew and Lizzie. Caroline jerked on her hand.

"Carry me, Avee. Me tired," the little girl pleaded. Avery hoisted her up and carried her back to the house. Her arms were aching by the time Caroline wiggled from her grasp to run inside with the others.

The children worked all morning decorating the tree with ribbons and pinecones, and Jake added a few candles to be lit when darkness fell.

Yikes, talk about a fire hazard! Avery thought, making a mental note to extinguish them as soon as the children went to bed.

Jake popped corn, declaring he wasn't useless in the kitchen, and Avery helped string it to add to the children's decorations. Her pile of popcorn dwindled as the children snuck handfuls to munch on each time they passed her place at the table, littering the ground with stray pieces.

"Jake, you're going to have to pop more corn. These three monkeys haven't left anything for the poor tree!" Avery wagged her finger at them. Jake started another batch while the children giggled unapologetically.

Once the tree was up in the main house, the children declared that Avery's cabin should be decorated as well. She consented to a few cedar boughs and ribbons around the windows, which did give the gloomy cabin a cheerier feel.

Avery spent little time in the cabin besides sleeping on the lumpy mattress (and she was so bone-tired from manual labor all day long that she really didn't mind it anymore), but she appreciated the children's thoughtfulness.

The first few nights, she had escaped from her handsome employer as soon as the children were tucked into bed, but one night he'd asked her to stay and have coffee with him. It had become something of a habit by now, though Avery had become partial to warm milk instead of Jake's coffee. Sometimes they chatted or read quietly before the fire (the bookworm in Avery thrilled at reading original versions of the very few books the family owned), and other times they played games at the kitchen table. Jake produced a set of checkers and a deck of cards. He taught her his favorite games, and she reciprocated.

Jake declared that he needed to get back to work, bringing her back to the present. The morning had turned out more than okay; Avery had found herself having a fabulous time. It was very different than Christmas decorating in the twenty-first century, but the sheer joy of the family spending time together and the homespun charm to the festive decorations left Avery feeling very warm inside.

Avery and the children spent the afternoon baking cookies in the wood-fired oven. It definitely took some trial and error, and the aftermath was a kitchen war zone of flour and sugar, but they had fun, nonetheless. She gave them each a spoon to lick the bowl clean while she tidied the mess and slid the last batch into the oven.

Later that evening, instead of taking the children upstairs, Jake gathered them around the sitting room. He lit the candles on the tree, while Avery eyed them nervously. Settling down in his seat, he arranged the large family Bible in his lap.

"You've heard the Christmas story many times, but it never gets too old to read about the Christ child, come to live among us and save the world from sin. It was a miracle of God's love, pure and simple, and a I'll read a bit of it from the Bible each night leading up to Christmas," Jake said.

The children, at least the older ones, seemed familiar with this and interjected their own thoughts and questions as he read about the angel foretelling the birth of Jesus.

"And in the sixth month the angel Gabriel was sent from God unto a city of Galilee, named Nazareth,

To a virgin espoused to a man whose name was Joseph, of the house of David; and the virgin's name was Mary.

And the angel came in unto her, and said, 'Hail, thou that art highly favoured, the Lord is with thee: blessed art thou among women."

As his rich, deep voice read from the first chapter

couldn't pass up the opportunity...especially at the thought of maybe dancing with the farmer beside her, who was turning out to be full of surprises.

"Yes, I think I'd like that very much," she answered.

∞∞∞

The day of the social arrived. Avery felt like a ball of nerves and wondered what she'd been thinking by agreeing to this madness, when Millie showed up at the house after lunch. She had her three girls in tow. The boys had stayed home to help their pa, much to Drew's disappointment. He soon stomped off to the barn to join Jake.

"I was feeling like a neighborly chat, and also wondered if you needed any help preparing for tonight?" Millie asked. Avery and Lizzie were up to their elbows in flour, attempting to bake a pie to contribute to the dessert table for the evening's festivities. It was not going very well, so they were more than happy to accept a bit of help from Millie. She was a seasoned veteran, and with a few directions from her, Avery soon had two edible-looking apple pies baking in the oven.

Millie settled baby Margaret on a pallet on the floor. The two women went to work cleaning up the kitchen while the older girls ran upstairs to play. They made small talk until Avery worked up the courage to ask what was really on her mind.

"Actually, Millie, I could use your help with

something. I'm not sure what's appropriate to wear tonight, and I'm hopeless at fixing my hair. I'd be grateful for any advice you could give me," she said.

"Oh dear, of course I can help you there! Let's go see what your options are." Once the pies were out of the oven and cooling, their delicious scent filling the air, the women and children trooped over to Avery's cabin. She stoked the fire and added a few sticks of firewood to warm the room, and then turned to the trunk that held her clothing. Avery had worn a few of the simple, sturdy day dresses she'd found near the top. She had avoided rummaging through the entire trunk, feeling strange about going through Kathleen's things.

Millie helped her remove each garment piece by piece and arranged them on the bed into two piles, one for everyday work wear and another for dressy occasions. There were very few in the second pile. Every once in a while, Millie would pull a dress out and smile with some unspoken memory or close her eyes and smell the fabric. Avery almost felt as if she was intruding on a private moment until Millie spoke.

"Kathleen was one of my best friends. I wasn't sure we would all make it after she passed, but time and grace have begun to heal us. Life is funny that way. But oh, I worried about Jake so, he was sad for such a long time…I wasn't sure about you at first, you know. When you arrived, well, it seemed a mite suspicious. You seemed to just come out of nowhere and we didn't know a thing about you, and you sure don't volunteer too much information about yourself.

"But, after seeing you with Kathleen's family the

Chapter 9

T he Cole family and Avery entered the church, where the Christmas social was being held. It was the only place in town large enough to ac- commodate the crowd of townspeople and outlying farm families that trickled in. It was Avery's first visit to the town's place of worship. She had declined each time Jake invited her to go along with the family.

Avery noted that somebody had worked very hard to give the humble structure a festive air. The smell of cedar filled the air as garlands trimmed with red ribbon hung on each wall. Tables covered in bright cloths, laden with food, were at one end of the room. Wooden pews had been moved aside, creating seating along the walls and an open space in the center of the room. A band warmed up at the far end and friends gathered in groups to visit with one another.

The children immediately spotted friends and ran to join the group of youngsters while Avery placed her pies on the dessert table. Friends and neighbors surged toward Jake in greeting and were happy to meet the mysterious Miss Lawson. Avery felt a bit like a goldfish in a bowl with all the attention, but the folks were warm and friendly, if just a smidge overly curious about her. She did a lot of smiling and nodding as dozens of people introduced themselves.

Avery breathed a sigh of relief when Zachary and Millie walked in and joined them. The crowd around them finally dispersed and soon they were sampling the various goodies heaped on the food tables. They kept close eyes on the children, who were beginning to get very rowdy with all the excitement.

When the music started up, Jake asked Avery if she'd like to dance.

"Oh, I don't know, Jake...I'm not much of a dancer," she began.

But Millie urged her on, assuring them she would keep Caroline out of trouble, and Avery soon found herself swept up in Jake's arms.

Avery told the truth when she said she didn't dance, so she felt nervous as someone began to call out instructions for the folk dance.

"Someone told me once not to worry and just laugh your way through it," Jake whispered close to her, and with that they were off and dancing, twirling, switching partners and circling through the room.

Avery missed the steps and stumbled several times, but so did lots of other people, including Jake. Soon she was laughing and enjoying herself immensely...especially the times when she was partnered with Jake. Truthfully, he wasn't a very good dancer either, but he enjoyed making fun of himself and had Avery in stitches each time they danced together.

come their norm, and she ignored his puzzled look at her early departure. *You really are a chicken,* she thought, tormenting herself.

However, she soon discovered that trying to sleep was futile. Her thoughts were like a freight train pummeling through her brain, torturously unrelenting.

It wasn't just Caroline, although the little girl was the largest part of her troubled thoughts. She was also thinking of and missing her parents terribly, the old hurt having come to the surface again. On some days she felt completely fine and content, lulled into the false sense that she was moving on with her life. But then a dark moment would sneak up on her when she least expected it, and grief would crash down on top of her like an all-consuming wave, so powerfully she could scarcely breathe.

Why do these things happen, these tragedies that rip hearts out and leave me, Jake—whoever—standing with the pieces? I've tried to pick them up and move on, but find myself so changed that the person I've become is unrecognizable from the girl I once was. And how are we supposed to move on to a new normal...to a new happiness?

She thought of Jake. She knew he was devastated when Kathleen died. But he seemed to have found his way again, as best as could be expected for someone coping with such a loss. He was a wonderful father and friend, but did he also have moments of hopelessness? By all appearances, he seemed to have figured out that balance of toughening up and moving on with life without giving in to cynicism. But what would it do to him if he lost Caroline? Avery imagined his despair and simply couldn't bear it.

Sighing again, she wondered what time it was. Goodness, she was going to have to go to the outhouse again. She needed to find a chamber pot to keep in her house like the children used at night.

Dragging on her boots and wrapping a thick blanket around herself, she made the cold trek out back. But on her return to the cabin, she glanced at the barn and noticed a light shining through the cracks. Curious, she changed course and soon pushed open the heavy door.

Jake turned at the sound.

"Oh, hello there. Thought you were one of the little'uns out of bed. What are you doing awake at this..." Jake's voice trailed off, his eyebrows rising in shock at the sight of her.

"What on earth are you wearing?" Ordinarily he had more tact, but she had obviously surprised him. Avery's eyes flew down as she noticed the blanket blowing in the breeze of the barn doorway, exposing the long johns she was wearing as pajamas. *His* long johns, she realized. Avery felt herself redden all over as she quickly stepped in the barn and wrapped herself up tightly.

"For your information, nightgowns are extremely uncomfortable," she muttered to the floor. Peeking up at Jake, she saw he was blushing too, and from all appearances, trying to hold back his grin.

"Anyway, what are you doing up?" she changed the subject, gesturing to him as he sat perched on a stool next to a large, brown cow.

she'd tried to run away from him and rely only on herself. He was always there, loving her, directing her path to rather unexpected places, and waiting for her to return to him.

Jake watched the emotions play over her face, the sadness that had been just below the surface melting away into joy. He reached for her and she leaned into his embrace.

Right there on the barn floor, Jake prayed aloud over Avery, thanking God for the blessing she had been to his family, for the burden that had been lifted from her, and asking the Lord for strength. When he finished, she looked at him, knowing he could see the inner peace shining from her eyes.

Suddenly, they were interrupted by a very loud, "Moooooo!" They looked over to see the agitated cow struggling. Jake leapt into action. Avery watched, in equal parts horror and fascination, as he reached up into the cow and appeared to try and rearrange the calf's position before it could be born.

"All right, I might need some help here. I'm gonna pull this calf out. Think you can hold Mama's head steady there?"

Ummmm....no! Avery thought. But she moved across the straw anyway, gently stroked the cow's head, and placed a hand on each side.

"That's it, just like that. Now, brace yourself!" He began to pull from his end, while Avery attempted to keep the cow steady and calm.

"Shhh...you're okay. It's gonna be all right. Jake knows what to do," she whispered, hoping it was true as the cow let out a disapproving noise. Avery glanced up at Jake to see him struggling, and then a slippery, wet baby calf emerged. The cow relaxed and Jake laughed, holding the soppy bundle in his arms.

"Welcome to the world, little fella," he said. The calf blinked in a mixture of confusion and wonder at his new surroundings. Avery couldn't help but smile at the whole disgusting, miraculous process that had brought the calf into the world.

"See? New life...one of the good things," Jake said as he stood, still holding the calf. He walked to a clean stall with fresh straw and laid the little guy down. Then he returned and led the mother cow to meet the baby.

"Let's leave them alone for a bit," he said, closing the gate and going to wash up over a clean bucket of water.

"That was amazing!" Avery said. "I've never been a part of anything like that in my life."

"It never gets old for me, either," Jake replied. They walked back over to the stall and peeked to see the new mother and baby getting acquainted.

∞∞∞

"Jake, there's something I need to talk to you about," Avery began. Jake turned away from the stall. The little calf was now feeding eagerly, and he was confident mama and baby were going to be just fine. That, coupled with Avery's revelations, left him feeling light-

shed tears as she thought about saying goodbye to the children she had come to love. Would Jake even allow her that?

Her heart thumped at the thought of the man himself. Now that she was leaving, she could admit that she had come to care for him far too much. Avery closed her eyes and thought about the thrill of his arms around her as they had danced and laughed together... had that been only two days ago?

There was a sudden knock at the door as Avery was folding and putting away Kathleen's borrowed clothes. Surely Jake didn't expect to take her to town this soon? It was barely dawn.

Curiously, Avery opened the door. Bundled up against the cold, Jake stood there, looking grim and like he had had anything but a restful night. He no longer looked angry, but rather resigned. Avery resisted the impulse to reach up and stroke his rough cheek.

"A tree limb fell on the fence and the cattle have gotten out. I'm going to have to ride out to round them up and repair the fence. It will probably take most of the day. I know what we talked about last night, and what I said still stands, but I'm afraid I've got to ask you if you could watch the children one last time today. It looks like there's a storm brewing and I just don't want them to be alone today," he blurted out, barely taking a breath.

Avery felt her heart leap. "Of course," she said softly. "I'll go over right now."

∞∞∞

Jake reached out and put a hand on the house-keeper's arm as she left the cabin, blocking her path momentarily. It had taken every ounce of his strength to trek over to the cabin and ask her to stay with the children, and he still questioned the wisdom of such a decision.

"I really am sorry that it has to be this way. I know the children will miss you terribly," he said hoarsely. He didn't add that he would miss her too, or that he had been awake most of the night thinking about what she had said about Caroline. As soon as he had come into the house from the barn, he checked on each of the children, and then lifted the sleeping Caroline out of her bed and brought her to his. He spent most of the night watching her sleep, making sure she was okay. When he had seen the look of the sky and the broken fence that morning, he knew he couldn't leave the children alone today if there was even the slightest chance that what Avery had said were true. He had even planned on staying with them all day himself, but now he couldn't do that with their whole livelihood loose on the prairie, and it was out of the question to take Caroline on such a rescue. He knew Avery was most likely insane, but he no longer questioned that she loved his children as her own.

"Okay, Caroline, I'm going to get you! If you make it to Lizzie and Drew before I do, you win!" Avery tried to keep her voice light, as though she were playing a game. She took a deep breath and another tentative step. The ice held, and Avery began running toward the little girl. Shrieking with delight, Caroline hastily took off toward her siblings.

Avery felt her heart leap with joy as Caroline ran off the pond and into Lizzie's waiting arms. She slowed down, breathing a huge sigh of relief.

Crack! Little fractures began forming near Avery's feet. *Oh no, no, no,* she thought as she frantically tried to reach the bank. There was one last, earsplitting crack and Avery's own scream as the ice gave way and she plunged into the freezing water.

∞∞∞

Jake rounded the corner of the barn. He saw that the children had been playing in the snow near the house, taking note of the footprints and half-finished snowmen. *They must have gotten cold and gone inside,* he thought. But then he heard the shouting. What were they doing over by the pond?

They came into view just as Caroline was leaping into Lizzie's arms. Why was Avery standing on the ice— had the woman lost her senses completely?

"Avery, no!" he shouted as the ice cracked and she frantically tried to reach the edge. He was already running when she went under. Mercifully, a coil of rope dangled from the fence post and he grabbed it as he ran past. Drew and Lizzie were screaming frantically. Jake hurriedly tied the rope to a tree trunk and slid onto the ice. Dropping to his stomach and scooting to the edge of the broken ice, he mentally urged Avery to fight.

As soon as she'd hit the water, Avery had felt the cold stabbing her like knives. Her muscles seized up and she thought about how ironic it was that all this time she was trying to prevent Caroline's death, and now Avery's own name might replace hers in the family Bible. She saw all their faces—Lizzie, Drew, Caroline, and finally their daddy. She pictured Jake's smiling face, the way his eyes crinkled when he laughed and how that muscle near his mouth twitched when he was teasing her. She felt the warmth of him against her back when he took her out riding and the way his light brown eyes twinkled as he spun her around in a dance. Jake, the man who had suddenly become such a big part of her life and who she now realized that she loved with all her heart.

No! I'm not going to die today, a small voice inside her cried. With all her strength, she willed her legs to kick and her arms to reach up to the surface. She was able to get one breath of air, hearing cries of her name, before she plunged under again to the quiet below. Her soaked dress weighed her down, pulling her toward the bottom of the pond. *Fight!* she urged, but felt it was a

thought, trying to breathe normally as she imagined what it must have taken to save her life. At the moment she felt extremely warm all over, with a mixture of embarrassment and wonder. Carefully, she sat up, seeing that she had slept on the floor before the fire. From the indention of blankets next to her, she hadn't been alone.

There was a crash from the kitchen, and Avery turned to see that Jake had dropped whatever dish he'd been holding.

"Avery," he whispered and ran to her. Kneeling on the floor, he pulled her into a bone-crushing hug. She sank into him, feeling that a part of her remembered him holding her all night and keeping her safe. Jake pulled away to look in her face, stroking her hair and cheeks.

"I thought I was going to lose you," he said. "Thank God you're all right."

"Jake, I..."

"Wait, let me say this. I'm so sorry about everything. I believe you, impossible as it all is. You saved Caroline—Lizzie and Drew explained what happened. I can't thank you enough for saving my little girl, even though it put you in such danger and nearly cost your life." Jake's voice broke as he wiped at the tears forming in his eyes.

He continued, "You were right, and I was wrong to try and send you away. You belong here, with the children...with me." Jake searched her eyes tenderly.

"Avery, I love you. I know it's not fair of me to ask, but please...please stay with me." Avery's bright green eyes met his honey brown ones. He loved her. And he believed her? Believed the impossible situation that had brought her here? And more than that, he wanted her to stay. Avery closed her eyes and thought of the life she had left behind. Could she really abandon her own time and stay in the nineteenth century indefinitely? What was she willing to give up in order to be with Jake and the children?

Avery opened her eyes and met Jake's questioning gaze. She imagined a future without him and the children, but it seemed such an empty darkness. What she'd be giving up was rather irrelevant. This man had lit the path for her in her darkest hours and helped her find peace. And then he saved her when she was at death's door. A life with him by her side was all she ever wanted or needed. Nobody could ever know what the future held, but they would face it together. She sighed with sheer joy and nodded slowly.

"Oh, Jake, yes. More than anything, I want to stay...with you," Avery pulled him closer to her, and his golden eyes danced with merriment.

"Did you know I was trying to say something when you pulled me out?" she asked. Jake shook his head.

"My heart was saying it, and my voice was trying to, but I couldn't make the words come out," she continued.

"You were nearly unconscious, love," he reminded her.

"I know, but it was so frustrating to know I might die before I got to say, 'I love you,'" she finished. Jake's face split into a huge smile.

"Is that right?" The old, lighthearted Jake was back.

"Yes, that's right!" Avery grinned, feeling like her heart would burst from happiness. Jake brushed a stray lock of hair from her eyes, cupped her cheek in his work-roughened hands and tenderly, tentatively their lips met. The kiss was gentle, and he seemed afraid she'd break after the ordeal she'd been through. But it deepened as she wrapped her arms around his strong chest, and he pulled her closer.

Avery felt a fire light inside her that she didn't know she possessed, and she let herself sweetly drown in his kisses as he worked his hands into her tangle of hair. However, they were stopped from losing their senses completely as they heard an opening door and three pairs of feet clambering down the stairs. They pulled away from each other, breathless, but Jake kept one arm around her shoulder as they sat together on the floor and winked playfully.

"I think I'm gonna have to share you," he said, as Lizzie, Drew and Caroline came into view. Their eyes lit up to see that Avery was awake and well. Running to the couple sitting on the floor, the kids jumped into their laps and there were hugs and kisses all around until the five of them collapsed, laughing, into one big, happy pile of blankets and family and heaps of love.

Epilogue

Avery tightly clutched the hand-written note in one hand and Kathleen's journal in the other as she walked briskly toward the barn. So much had transpired in the last few days that she could hardly believe it was real. After her ordeal, Jake had scarcely let her out of his sight. She stayed in the main house for two days while he waited on her hand and foot. He took her to his bed and insisted she sleep there, while he, ever the gentleman, slept in the cabin next door.

Of course, the children were happy to have Avery well and close by, and they spent their time vying for her attention. She and Jake had spent many long hours after the children were asleep each evening talking about everything under the sun. She revealed life as she knew it in the twenty-first century, little bits at a time so as not to overwhelm him. He was completely fascinated by it, especially when she explained things like automobiles and telephones. In turn, he told her all about his childhood in Ohio, making history come alive right before her very eyes.

Jake explained all of his dreams for the farm and future cattle ranch, while Avery excitedly told him of her university courses in business. He was astonished that women of the future attended the same colleges and attained equal degrees as men, but he admitted that she gave knowledgeable suggestions to help start the cattle operation as they discussed ideas back and forth.

My education just might come in handy, after all—with this family business, Avery thought. Jake voiced the same idea, and the two grinned at one another.

When Christmas morning came, they all gathered around the tree, and this time it was Avery who read aloud her favorite part of the Christmas story, from Luke chapter two.

"And she brought forth her firstborn son, and wrapped him in swaddling clothes, and laid him in a manger; because there was no room for them in the inn.

And there were in the same country shepherds abiding in the field, keeping watch over their flock by night.

And, lo, the angel of the Lord came upon them, and the glory of the Lord shone round about them; and they were sore afraid.

And the angel said unto them, 'Fear not: for, behold, I bring you good tidings of great joy, which shall be to all people.

For unto you is born this day in the city of David a Saviour, which is Christ the Lord.'

And suddenly there was with the angel a multitude of the heavenly host praising God, and saying,

'Glory to God in the highest, and on earth peace, good will toward men.'"

The children fidgeted, eager to open their presents, but Avery and Jake were both filled with joy at the ancient, holy words she read.

Later, the couple sat on the couch together, holding hands. They watched the youngsters open their gifts, listening to their exclamations of glee over the new toys and candy. "I have something for you," Jake said, reaching behind him and pulling out a small parcel. Questioningly, Avery tore the paper off, revealing a small box. When she opened it, she saw a beautiful, oval-shaped locket inside. It was pewter-colored, with a filigree pattern encircling a rose in the center. Avery recognized it as one she had admired the first time Jake took her to the mercantile in town.

"Oh Jake, I love it!" She pulled the necklace out and Jake hooked the clasp around her neck.

"I'm glad. I went back to Whitnash's as soon as I could after I saw that you seemed rather taken with it," he explained. "It looks perfect on you," he said.

Avery was having the best Christmas she could remember, so when the children ran off to play and she turned back to Jake, she was surprised to see a pained look cross his face.

"What's wrong?" she asked, alarmed.

"I've been thinking," he began.

"Well, there's your first problem," she quipped, but seeing he wasn't in a joking mood, she turned her full attention on him.

"What is it?"

"You're not from this time, and it's selfish and unfair of me to ask you to stay. If you want to go home, to the future, I can help you. We'll figure out a way. It has something to do with the trunk and the journal, maybe if we—"

"No, Jake," she said, cutting him off. "I've had a lot of time to think the last few days, and I meant what I said. I want to stay with you, more than anything. I love you. I know what waits for me there and it doesn't hold a candle to what I have here. This is where I want to be," Avery said, cradling both of his cheeks in her hands and looking straight into his light brown eyes, the flecks of gold catching the candlelight.

"Really?" he asked.

"Yes, really. I promise," she replied. His hands curled around hers and he closed his eyes, the worry lines fading away.

"Well, in that case," he said, dipping his head and kissing her softly and slowly. His kisses made their way from her mouth and across her cheek, and his whiskers tickled her ear.

"Marry me?" he whispered to her. She pulled back so she could look him in the eye, and felt a huge smile spread across her face as she nodded.

"Yes. Yes, I will!"

"Whoop!" he yelled, grinning and lifting her in

Made in the USA
Las Vegas, NV
30 November 2020